Tom Turkey

David M. Sargent, Jr., and his friends live in Northwest Arkansas. His writing career began in 1995 with a cruel joke being played on his mother. The friends pictured with him are (from left to right), Vera, Buffy, and Mary.

Dave Sargent is a lifelong resident of the small town of Prairie Grove, Arkansas. A fourth-generation dairy farmer, Dave began writing in early December, 1990. He enjoys the outdoors and has a real love for birds and animals.

Tom Turkey

By

Dave Sargent

Illustrated by
Jane Lenoir

Ozark Publishing, Inc.
P.O. Box 228
Prairie Grove, AR 72753

Library of Congress cataloging-in-publication data

Sargent, Dave, 1941—
Tom Turkey / by Dave Sargent ; illustrated by Jane Lenoir.
p. cm.
Summary: Tom Turkey is shocked at the naughty behavior of a young siamese kitten named Samone, who thinks that she can bully everyone arond, but Samone is in for a big suprise. Includes nonfiction information about turkeys.
ISBN 1-56763-475-3(cb) -- ISBN 1-56764-476-1 (pbk.)
[1. Turkeys--Fiction. 2. Cats--Fiction. 3. Bullies--Fiction.] I. Lenoir, Jane, 1950- ill. II. Title.

PZ7.S2465 To 2000
[Fic]--dc21

00-024838

Printed in the United States of America

Inspired by

watching turkeys as they strut along, with their chests thrown out and their heads held high. You can tell by the way they carry themselves, they are proud birds.

Dedicated to

all students who love to watch turkeys strut along.

Foreword

Tom Turkey is shocked at the bullish attitude of a young Siamese kitten named Samone. She thinks she can boss everyone around. But Samone has a big surprise coming!

Contents

Tom Turkey

If you would like to have an author of The Feather Tale Series visit your school, free of charge, just call 1-800-321-5671 or 1-800-960-3876.

One

Tom Meets Samone

The morning air was filled with the fresh scent of new foliage and flowers. Molly stepped from the porch into the pleasant warmth of the sunshine and smiled.

"What a beautiful spring day," she murmured. "It will be a perfect day to clean house and work in my flower garden."

She stood there gazing at the beauty of the countryside for several moments before going back into the house. You know, I really like Molly,

Tom Turkey thought as he watched the door close behind her. She's always happy. Big Tom ruffled the feathers on his massive body and puffed out his chest. He held his bald, bluish colored head in a proud position as he strutted back and forth, patiently waiting for Molly to return.

A short time later, Molly and Farmer John came out of the house. Molly was carrying something that she had found sleeping with Barney.

"I think this is a good day to introduce Samone the Siamese Kitten to the farm, don't you, John?" she said with a chuckle.

"Now, Molly, you know she was born in my daddy's old barn. I'm sure she already knows the animals and her way around this big farm," Farmer John replied with a smile.

Tom watched as Molly carefully sat the little brown and tan feline on the ground. The kitten purred and rubbed against Molly's leg, but her blue eyes stared at the big turkey.

Hmmm, Tom thought. Maybe I can help that little kitten feel more at home in the barnyard.

Although Tom Turkey's glossy brown feathers, long red wattles, and enormous feet seemed to demand respect from the other animals on the farm, Samone the Siamese Kitten glared scornfully at him. He turned his attention back to Molly.

Molly said with a smile, "John, the ladies in the Garden Club will be here tomorrow for lunch and to see my prize winning rose bush. I want everything to look nice for them."

As Molly returned to the house, Farmer John got in his truck and drove away. Tom looked at the little feline again and smiled.

"It's such a great day," he said. "I just love springtime, don't you?"

“Oh, yeah,” the kitten replied with a sneer. “It’s the perfect time of the year to let everyone on this farm know who’s boss!”

"And," Tom Turkey drawled, "just who might that be?"

"Why me, of course," Samone snarled, with her claws extented.

The turkey paced back and forth in front of the kitten for a moment before asking, "And who appointed you boss over the farm?"

"Why nobody!" Samone yelled. "I set the rules. I also enforce them. And all of you better follow them!"

Man alive! When Samone the cute little Siamese Kitten spoke these words, Tom Turkey's head suddenly turned bright red, and his wingtips dug into the ground.

"Gobble, gobble," he bellowed. "You may look like a nice little Siamese kitten, but your heart is as cold and fierce as a hungry tiger! You are a little bully!" he growled.

“Yeah, I am,” Samone sneered. “Bullying others is what I do best.”

Tom Turkey stomped his foot and bellowed, "If you continue to be so obnoxious, you won't have any friends!"

"Good," young Samone snarled. "I'm lazy and I don't like to work. My mama knows I'm lazy! I don't even listen to her! I'd much rather be boss, and a boss doesn't need friends, just quiet and obedient followers."

Barney the Bear Killer walked around the house and grinned at Tom.

"Barney, come here," Tom said. "I would like to introduce you to the newest member of the family."

Within a split second, Samone raced up the nearest tree and onto a low branch hanging directly over the unsuspecting dog and leaped down.

"Ouch!" Barney yelped as the cat's claws dug into his back.

"You better get back in your dog house," the Siamese kitten screamed.

Barney thought that he and the little kitten were becoming friends, but now, he wasn't sure. He glanced at Tom, but the turkey only shrugged.

"I don't know what to do with her, Barney. That kitten is headed for trouble!" Tom said as they watched Samone race around the corner of the house and disappear.

"You're right," Barney agreed, "She's starting off on the wrong foot! That's no way to act when you need or want to make new friends."

"I'm going to try to keep her safe for Molly's sake," Tom said. "She thinks that kitten is special."

Suddenly a loud crash sent the turkey scurrying around the house.

"Wish me luck, Barney," he gobbled over his shoulder. "That ornery little kitten is a rascal!"

The huge bird was halfway across the yard when he again heard the kitten.

“I’m the new boss,” Samone screamed. “Now, you get out of this yard and stay out!”

Two

Samone Turns Tiger!

Tom gulped as he gazed at the bird feeder. It was lying on the ground, bent and broken. Samone grinned and raced to the front porch. Molly had placed her knitting basket on the porch swing while she cleaned the living room. Throw rugs hung over the banister, and a broom and mop were leaned against the wall beside the front door. Tom heard the vacuum cleaner running, which explained why she did not know about the bird feeder yet.

"Samone!" Tom yelled. "You have done enough damage for one morning."

"You aren't my boss. You are just a big feather duster with legs." the little critter snarled.

Tom stomped his big foot and yelled, "Stop acting like such a bully! You have a naughty, nasty attitude."

The kitten suddenly leaped from the porch steps onto one of the rugs. As it slid to the ground, she jumped to the next one, and it, too, fell in a heap on top of the rose bush.

"Wow!" she giggled. "Hey! This is fun!"

Then Samone noticed a small squirrel peeking at her from a short distance away.

"Meoww!" she growled as she lunged at the little critter.

The frightened squirrel circled the yard once before bounding onto the porch with Samone nipping at Suzie Squirrel's bushy tail.

They raced across the swing, knocking the basket, balls of yarn, and knitting needles onto the deck. Another circle around the porch knocked the broom and mop across the doorway. As the squirrel veered off the porch, Molly opened the door and fell over the mop and broom.

For a moment, Tom and Samone just stared at Molly. Finally, she groaned and struggled to stand up, but her right ankle was hurt. She gently rubbed her face with one hand, and Tom noticed that her left eye had been bruised by the fall. Suddenly Tom Turkey heard a truck approaching the house. Thank goodness, he thought. Molly needs help.

As the truck door slammed shut, he saw Farmer John running toward the porch.

"Molly!" he yelled. "What in tarnation happened? Are you okay?"

"I fell over the broom, John," she said weakly. "I think my ankle is broken or sprained."

He glanced around at the broken bird feeder, balls of yarn, scattered needles, rugs, and overturned mop and broom as he hurried up the steps.

"Who did all this damage?" he yelled angrily. "I'll deal with them later!"

"I think Samone was playing on the porch," Molly murmured.

Moments later, the truck was roaring down the lane to the hospital.

As silence replaced the roar of the speeding vehicle, Tom ruffled his feathers and asked, "Now, Samone, who are you going to bully? You just hurt the lady who feeds you!" But Samone was nowhere to be seen.

Tom Turkey heard a strange sound. Barney the Bear Killer was running back and forth across the yard. The black and tan coonhound had his nose close to the ground, and Tom was hearing his heavy sniffing.

"Can you find her?" Tom asked.

The dog did not raise his nose from the ground, but a wag of his tail told of his intentions. Tom fell into step behind Barney. He traced every move the dog made as he moved ever nearer to the barn. Suddenly Barney stopped and raised his right paw.

"So," Tom said quietly. "She's in the barn, huh? Thanks, Barney."

As the coonhound trotted back to the house, Tom entered the barn. The kitten was leaning against a bale of hay. Her shoulders quivered, and her sobs echoed within the quiet of the barn. Tom watched the kitten cry.

"Molly will be fine," he said quietly. "Don't cry, Samone."

"I didn't m - mean to h - hurt anybody," the kitten mewed. "I was just having fun."

"I know," the turkey murmured as he patted Samone on the back with one wing. "This is a high price to pay for being a bully, isn't it?"

The little kitten hiccuped and nodded her head before going into another spasm of sobs.

"I'm g - going to live in the barn for the r - rest of my l - life," she wailed, "b - because I d - don't deserve to l - live with M - Molly."

Tom paced thoughtfully back and forth for a long time. Samone wiped a tear from her eye, then sat up to watch him. She sniffled as the big bird muttered to himself.

"Hmmm. And hmmm. Yes. That just might work."

Suddenly, Tom stopped pacing and whirled around to face the little kitten. The unexpected move caused Samone to lose her balance and fall over onto her back.

"Do you want to undomost of the damage that you have done?" Tom asked sternly.

"Y - y - yes," the kitten mewed.

"Very well," the turkey replied. "I have a plan, but you must work very hard and very very fast. Are you willing to do this?"

The kitten nodded agreement and said, "I will work hard and fast, Tom, and I will never bully anybody again."

"Good," Tom said. "Then listen closely. You must hurry and . . ."

Three

Tom Teaches Samone

Samone flew into action. Her paws worked feverishly rewinding balls of yarn and gathering knitting needles. She apologized to all the onlookers as she carefully arranged the yarn in the knitting basket. She told of her intent to be a good friend as she repaired and rehung the bird feeder in the tree. She spoke of fun times together as she shook the rugs and positioned them inside the house. She purred as she moved the mop and broom into the utility closet.

"And," she assured her audience as she put the neat knitting basket beside Molly's recliner, "I will never ever ever bully anybody again!"

Suddenly, Farmer John's truck rolled into the driveway, and the farm animals headed for the trees, bushes, and barnyard.

"The doctor said I'll be fine, John." Molly said as she slowly hobbled from the truck toward the house. "In a few days, no one will even notice my minor injuries. Of course, I'll have to delay my luncheon for the Garden Club and clean up this . . ."

"Why, look, Molly. The mess has already been cleaned up," he said with a chuckle. "I'll carry everything back into the house. You just rest."

Tom looked at Samone, and the kitten nodded.

"I'll go in and sit on her lap," she whispered. "My purr and loving disposition will tell her that I'm not a bully anymore."

Tom agreed as he walked across the drive toward the barnyard.

I believe, he thought, that tiger has been tamed. Her bullying days are over. He glanced back at Samone who was curled up on Molly's lap.

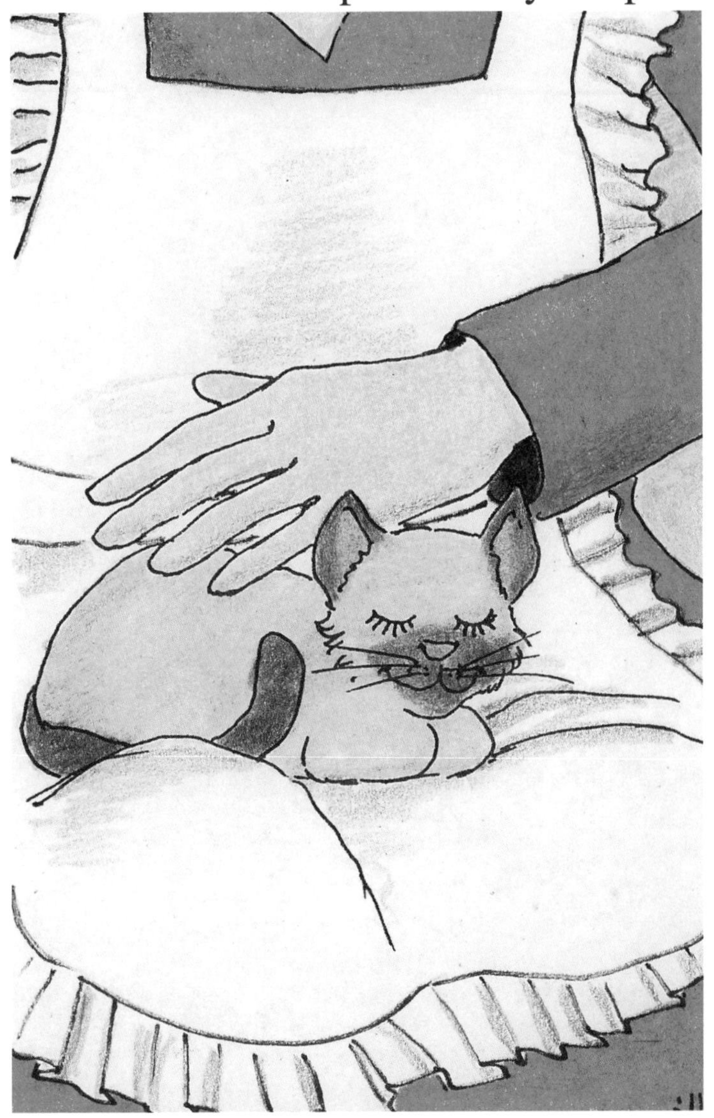

“I’m sure,” he groaned softly. “that her bullying days are past, aren’t they?” Hmmm . . .

Four

Turkey Facts

Turkey is a common name for two large American birds. In adult turkeys the head and neck are essentially naked, the feathers being reduced to hairlike bristles. The tarsus is equipped with spurs, and the tail feathers can be raised to form a vertical fan during courtship or aggressive displays. Like many other members of the order to which they belong, turkeys are polygamous; the cocks fight among themselves for access to the hens.

The nests are built of dried leaves and grasses in concealed places on the ground. From nine to eighteen creamy white eggs with red-brown speckles are laid in a clutch.

The wild turkey, native to northern Mexico and the eastern United States, is the species from which all domesticated breeds have been developed. The female bird has buff-colored feathers on the tips of the wing coverts and on the tail.

The male has a long wattle at the base of the bill and additional wattles on the neck, as well as a prominent tuft of bristles resembling a beard projecting downward from its chest.

The wild turkey, once exterminated in much of its range through hunting and habitat loss, made an excellent comeback in the mid-20th century, occupying most of its original range; it has also been successfully introduced into Hawaii and some parts of the western United States where it did not formerly occur. It was originally domesticated in Mexico, and was brought into Europe early in the 16th century. Since that time, turkeys have been extensively raised because of the excellent quality of their meat and eggs. Common breeds of turkey in the United States are the Bronze, Narragansett, White Holland, and Bourbon Red. About 240 million turkeys are raised each year in the United States, with North Carolina,

Minnesota, and California leading in production.

The ocellated turkey is native to the Yucatán Peninsula of Mexico and adjacent Guatemala and Belize. The tail feathers have green-blue eye-spots and an iridescent purple cast. The body feathers have a metallic golden, bronze-green sheen. The skin of both the head and neck is blue and is covered with red, wartlike growths.

Scientific Classification: Turkeys belong to the family *Phasianidae* of the order *Galliformes.* They are sometimes placed in a separate family called *Meleagrididae.* The wild turkey is classified as *Meleagris gallopavo* and the ocellated turkey as *Agriocharis ocellata.*